Interchange

AMY LAURENS

OTHER WORKS

SANCTUARY SERIES

Where Shadows Rise
Through Roads Between
When Worlds Collide

KADITEOS SERIES

How Not To Acquire A Castle
How Not To Ring The Hero's Bell
How Not To Take Over The World

SHORT STORY COLLECTIONS

Of Sea Foam and Blood
Darkness and Good

NON-FICTION

How To Write Dogs
How To Theme
How To Create Cultures
How To Create Life
How To Map (2019/20)

Find other works by the author at
www.amylaurens.com

Interchange

INKLET #21

AMY LAURENS

Inkprint
PRESS

www.inkprintpress.com

This is a work of fiction. All characters, organisations and events are the author's creation, or are used fictitiously.

Print ISBN: 978-1-925825-21-3
eBook ISBN: 9781386323563

www.inkprintpress.com

National Library of Australia Cataloguing-in-Publication Data
Laurens, Amy 1985 –
Interchange
36 p.
ISBN: 978-1-925825-21-3
Inkprint Press, Canberra, Australia
1. Young Adult Fiction—Coming of Age 2. Young Adult Fiction—Social Themes—New Experience 3. Young Adult Fiction—Health & Daily Living—Diseases, Illness & Injuries

First Print Edition: November 2019
Cover design © Inkprint Press
Interior art © Amy Laurens

INTERCHANGE

"THAT'S RIDICULOUS, JAMES!" ELLA said into her mobile, grateful there was no one else at the bus stop to hear her. The traffic whooshed past on the four-lane road, kicked up the smell of hot asphalt and petrol fumes. "I think I'm capable of running my own life, thanks." She glanced up at the approaching bus juddering its way toward her—an old one, all orange and sky blue. "Look," she said. "I've got to go. I've *no* doubt we'll discuss this later. Bye."

She hung up on James, thinking as she did how irritating he was becoming. This was the third time he'd expressed disapproval over her plans to go down the coast the weekend before exams. As if the break wouldn't settle her nerves. She shook her head in disgust.

The bus doors hissed open as it stopped, sending the smell of oil and hot hydraulics into the back of Ella's throat as she stepped up inside.

"Student, please," she said curtly. Ignoring the driver's brief glance at her cleavage, she scanned the bus for an empty seat. The bus stank of old sweat and musty upholstery, nearly full with students and old folk on the way home from bingo. And of course, the occasional middle-aged drifter, taking up space. And leering, like they had the chance to do anything more than look. Ella snorted in disgust.

She spied a seat, halfway down on the left side, and swept down the aisle, flinging herself onto the worn blue seat and wishing, yet again, that she could afford a car.

Scooting over against the window, her thoughts returned to James.

How dare he, she thought. *It's my life, it's my money, I can go away if and when I please, thank you very much.*

Perhaps it was time for a change. She'd been seeing James for what, like two months now? She nodded to herself. That guy in her English class was pretty cute. *Ben. I think he's Ben.*

The bus arrived at the interchange, interrupting her musings. Half of the passengers disembarked and a new horde of students climbed on to take their place.

The last passenger caused Ella to wrinkle her nose—yet another middle-aged man. Briefly, she wondered why there were so many of them on the buses.

Why do these losers not have cars?

The latest specimen headed her way and realisation hit her: the only free seat left was next to her.

She set her handbag firmly on the seat, and shook her head. He didn't seem to see her.

He slid in without a word of apology, a skinny shell of a man taking up far less than half the seat.

The handbag sat like an immutable barrier between them. Ella stared resolutely out the window, hoping that her new companion didn't have too far to travel. She was a good half hour away from her stop, but if he was still there when she had to get off... Well, the last thing she needed was another middle-aged man staring at her butt.

She shuddered slightly at the thought, and examined him out of the corner of her eye. He didn't really look like the butt-staring type, but sometimes they didn't. He was on a bus, after all.

She was about to resume her internal rant at James when—horror of all horrors—the man began to cry. Just softly, and Ella looked around in a covert panic to see if anyone else had noticed.

No one else has noticed, he probably doesn't expect me *to notice, it's all okay, just ignore him.* She stared out the window.

Ella decided that he mustn't have any tissues, as she couldn't think of any other reason why he would sniff so horribly. For a moment, she almost felt sorry for him. Then she remembered that she still didn't know how far he was travelling, and the sympathy faded.

Soon enough, though, the man leaned forward to push the 'stop' button. The purple light up the front of the bus came on. Ella sagged in relief. No butt-staring after all.

She lurched forward as the bus jolted to a stop. The doors opened, and the purple light winked out. The man wiped his face and slid into the aisle.

The doors closed and the bus pulled back into the traffic before Ella glanced down, and noticed the black leather wallet on the seat.

Ella sat on her bed in her plain white t-shirt and pastel tartan pyjama shorts, stroking her tabby rescue cat and staring at the wallet. *To open, or not to open, that is the question*, she thought, proud of herself for actually remembering something from high school.

The scent of the oils in her Versace warmer filled the room, bright and fresh and sunshiney, somewhat at odds with her mood.

"Well, I can't keep it forever, can I, Smudge?" She scratched the tabbycat behind the ear and reached for the wallet.

It was soft, worn, and smelled pleasantly of treated leather.

The driver's licence revealed that the crying man was a Mr Edward Hampton, of Lilac Street, Watson.

Driver's licence? Ella wondered. *He has a licence?* "Why the heck was he on the bus then, Smudgie?" She shook her head, and continued shuffling.

Twenty dollars cash, healthcare card, bank card, credit card, photos of a woman with mid-length wavy brown hair—quite lovely—and a baby—round and pudgy, with brown fuzz instead of hair. Library card, Subway discount card—bus ticket.

Bus ticket.

"Smudge," Ella addressed the cat, holding him up to look into his eyes. "I'm puzzled. Why would anyone in their right mind catch a bus when they could drive? For that matter," she said, putting the cat down and gathering the cards back into the wallet, "why would someone catch a bus if they were going to cry?"

She lay back, staring at the poster on the far wall. "Well," she said, "looks like I'm off to Watson tomorrow. Down you go." She lifted the cat onto the floor, switched off her lamp and snuggled under the covers.

Ella knocked on the plain front door of the tiny house, crammed in elbow-to-elbow amid identical, grey-rendered neighbours, running through what she was going to say in her head. She still wasn't convinced this was the right thing to do—should have just handed it in to the bus company's lost property or some-thing—but she was filled with a curiosity she couldn't quite explain.

The woman from the photo ans-wered the door, with the baby on her hip. "Hello?"

"Hi," said Ella brightly, trying to hide her nerves. "My name's Ella. Mr

Hampton left his wallet on the bus yesterday." She held it out as proof.

The woman exhaled with relief. "Why thank you, Ella, that was thoughtful of you to return it."

Ella blushed. She fidgeted, wanting to ask, wanting to know—*Why he was crying? On a bus, of all places?*—but uncertain how to begin.

"Is there anything else?" the woman asked, friendly and welcoming.

"Um, well…" Ella faltered. "It's just that on the bus…" She sighed and met the woman's gaze. "Is he okay?"

The woman's smile disappeared. "He's dying."

Ella flung herself onto her king single bed and stared up at the ceiling.

Dying. The Man was Dying.

She thought in capitals, unable to better express the weight that she perceived in the situation. Megan stuck her head into the room— "Dinner's ready!"—but Ella just nodded absently.

Megan gave her an odd look, then retreated to galumph down the stairs, two at a time.

Dying.

Ella closed her eyes.

'What of?' she had blurted in shock. 'If you don't mind me asking, of course,' she added in a clumsy attempt to soften her bluntness.

'Cancer,' the woman had replied. 'Bowel cancer. We've known for a while, but we thought he was improving.' She looked away. 'He saw the doctors yesterday. He has about eight months left.'

"Dinner!" Dad yelled out from downstairs.

Sighing, Ella rolled over. As she did she brushed against the photo frame on her bedside table. James. She lifted the picture up and stared at it.

The bus chugged along, its uneven gait shaking Ella as she sat, lost in thoughts about the coming day's classes. As it pulled in to a stop, Ella glanced up with mild curiosity to see who would get on. Just one passenger at this stop, a middle-aged man.

Moron, Ella thought—and then caught herself. Silently, she amended it: *Maybe the car's broken, like the Hampton's,* she thought, hoping as she did that the Hamptons would be able to have theirs fixed soon.

She sighed as this new man passed her, smelling faintly of cheap men's deodorant as he did. *Maybe he's dying.*

The thrum of the engine droned into her head, numbing her from the world. She could see things through the windows, watch people as they went about their lives, but the noise was like a barrier between her and the outside world. Nothing reached her, nothing connected with her. Staring blankly she remembered again:

The woman—Viola—had invited her inside.

'How do you cope?' Ella had asked. 'How do you live, like, going through each day, knowing what the outcome's going to be, but, like, you have to do the boring, daily stuff anyhow?'

Viola stared into space for a moment. She came back with a small shake of her head. 'I don't know Ella. I really don't. I mean, I feel like I haven't even absorbed it yet, not really. And what choice do I have? Whatever happens, I still have little Josh here,' she bounced the baby on her lap, 'and I have a responsibility to him not to curl up and hide.' She sighed. 'I just don't know.'

The bus jerked to a halt and, grabbing her bag, Ella joined the queue of students waiting to exit. Ahead of her a guy with scraggly blonde hair hanging over his eyes jumped down the steps and turned, offering his hand to the girl behind him. The girl smiled shyly, and took his hand.

Nice to see chivalry isn't dead, Ella thought. And sighed. *Dead.*

She sat in her class, thinking. She hadn't heard a word the lecturer had said, but her pen hadn't stopped moving as she spilled out a torrent of words, attempting to make sense of what had happened in the last twenty-four hours.

Mr Hampton is dying. Dying. Why do I feel so shocked at that? People die, things die all the time... but dying... I'm dying. Sally's dying. Mum's dying, Dad's dying, even Megan is dying. Living is dying.

James is dying.

James is dying. Why do I care?

He loves me.

He's overprotective and irritating. He's smothering me, telling me what to do all the time.

He loves me, and wants to make me happy. And he smells like peaches.

He wants to be with me.

Do I want to be with him?

He's a nice guy. Clever. Protective.

He's dying.

…

One chance at love.

One first chance, anyway.

Am I wasting his?

Ella sighed deeply, and recalled again Viola's words—*I have a responsibility not to curl up and hide.*

She wrote a word in capitals on her page:

HIDING.

And underlined it.

<u>HIDING.</u>

Carefully, she amended it once more:

Stop <u>HIDING</u>.

The lecture finished, and en masse the students packed up and left, the scent of garlic bread and hot chips wafting in from the food court outside as the double doors swung in and out, in and out.

Ella sighed, and slammed her book closed. She slipped it into her bag, and left the room. Outside, she paused. Yes, or no?

Nerves tingling in her stomach, Ella dug out her phone and pulled up James's number. She stared, debating, finger hovering over the call button.

Stop hiding.

She pressed the button, and walked off down the corridor as it dialled.

Time to stop hiding.

THE MAKING OF
INTERCHANGE

Secret confession: this is an old, old story.

And gosh. I was so *young* when I wrote this. Can you tell?

I mean, it's not *quite* as whimsically naïve as my high-school fiction, but it's getting there.

I was in uni, so I'd finished a few short stories by the time I wrote this one. But I was still feeling my way through the idea of ending a story, of having character development without slipping into didacticism, and this narrative uncertainty on my part shows, I think.

But regardless, I *am* proud of this story, because it represented the fruit of a very specific period in my writing life—and in my inner life, because of course, when you write from the heart a story can't help but reflect some of your inner longings, your inner tur-moil—the inner demons that you're still busy battling.

This particular demon, I think, was one that we all face when we grow up: learning to set boundaries in our rela-tionships.

I mean, I wasn't in a relationship that needed boundary-setting in any specific way at the time. I was, in fact, probably engaged to my husband, if I have my timeline correct. But I'd been a very placid teen in many ways, one who lived in a boat that was rocking plenty on its own, thank you very much, so I never felt the need to do any boat-rocking of my own. I was, and fundamentally always will be, a peace-keeper and a mediator.

So while this wasn't necessarily about setting boundaries in my current romantic relationship, it was definitely about finding the courage to set boundaries around my emotional life in general; to be brave and own my life; to refuse to drift on somebody else's current or let indecision pressure me into a course of action that wasn't wholly my own.

This story also signalled, in many ways, the beginning of that era in my writing, corresponding roughly with my twenties, where I had a lot of trouble forgiving naïvety—because I had been naïve once, in a rather significant way, and it had almost cost me something that I valued highly, and I was struggling to forgive myself.

This shows in later stories I wrote during that time period, where I was not so kind to characters who demonstrated any sort of naïvety at all. In fact, they usually ended up dead.

At least here we can presume that, whatever Ella decided, she is happy.

DOWNLOAD YOUR FREE EBOOK

When you buy a print book from Inkprint Press, we like to say THANK YOU by offering you the ebook for free!

Please head to
www.inkprintpress.com/inklets/21/
and the use the coupon INK21LET to get your copy of this Inklet in epub AND mobi today!
(Coupon will only work once.)

OF SEA FOAM AND BLOOD: TO DUST

Sometimes running away is the hardest thing you can do. What I want, what I really want, is to turn around right now and plunge back into the midst of the Maliche, let their rotting, stinking bodies surround me, and kill as many as I can before I die. For Mum. For Dad. For Joss.

God, please let Joss get away. Mum and Dad might be gone, but please, please… save him. I left him climbing for a rooftop, and the Maliche can't climb, and he might be safe enough— but I have to run, and running is so, so hard when all you want to do is die.

I can't die though, not today. Today I have to live, because in my backpack, weighing me down like guilt, is the box. It's a perfect cube I can balance on one hand, sharp-edged and shined to perfection—a magic box, the only hope we have of stopping the Maliche forever. And I want to stop them more than anything else in the world, more than I want to die, because while there are Maliche, no one dies.

And so I run, heading north in a town that runs south towards the battle, running for life and death and salvation along a road whipped by the wind and smogged with dust.

From dust created, to dust returned. Only that's exactly it: with the Maliche on our doorstep, there is no return. I've seen the bodies they leave behind, twisted, gruesome things with flesh squeezed until the insides pop, left in the sun to ferment with a rictus of pain on their faces.

And the eyes. The eyes are the worst.

No. Running away is hard, but it must be done. Humanity needs to die.

Keep reading! Head to http://www.amylaurens.com/books/short-stories/of-sea-foam-and-blood/
to buy your copy now!

ABOUT THE AUTHOR

AMY LAURENS is an Australian author of fantasy fiction for all ages. Unlike Ella, she actually enjoys riding public transport; at least it means she can write or read while commuting, instead of having to concentrate on driving!

Amy has written a middle grade fantasy trilogy (the *Sanctuary* series), and the humorous fantasy *Kaditeos* series, starting with *How Not To Acquire A Castle*. If you like Terry Pratchett, you'll very likely enjoy the world of Kaditeos.

You can find out more about Amy at her website, www.amylaurens.com.

INKLET #007
SEVENTY
LIANA BROOKS

INKLET #008
A Final Request for Mercy
AMY LAURENS

INKLET #009
the kitten psychologist
vs
the kitten's owners
THEA VAN DIEPEN

INKLET #010
Answer the Question
AMY LAURENS

INKLET #011
Happily, Red
AMY LAURENS

INKLET #012
the kitten psychologist
tries to be patient
through email
THEA VAN DIEPEN

INKLET #013
DRAGON Tuesday
AMY LAURENS

INKLET #014
RED PLANET REFUGEES
LIANA BROOKS

INKLET #015
the kitten psychologist &
What The Kitten Did
THEA VAN DIEPEN

INKLET #016
Cherry Blossom
AMY LAURENS

INKLET #017
Alone
AMY LAURENS

INKLET #018
the kitten psychologist & The Kitten Come To A Conclusion
THEA VAN DIEPEN

INKLET #019
LEVEL NINE
LIANA BROOKS

INKLET #020
To Dust
AMY LAURENS

INKLET #021
Interchange
AMY LAURENS

INKLET #022
Emalia's Lanterns
LIANA BROOKS

INKLET #023
Dear Santa
AMY LAURENS

INKLET #024
The Quilt-Maker's Scrap
AMY L. LAURENS